A very odd job

Bob and Benny were out on their lawn painting a sign. Benny splashed on the colours and his brother Bob painted the words. It was a messy business, but they didn't mind mess.

When the paint was all gone, there was the sign, finished. It said:

BENNY AND BOB: ANY ODD JOBS

BOB AND BENNY: ODD JOBS ANY

'That's us,' Bob said. 'We're going to be odd job men, starting today.'

They fixed the sign to their front gate. Then Benny went back to clean up the lawn, and Bob went into the kitchen to wash their jumpers.

That was when Mrs Catkin came along and saw their sign. She lived in a big house at the top of the village. It looked very grand, but inside it was rather ramshackle. This was because of Daisy, Mrs Catkin's pet elephant. Daisy was only a baby, but she was rather a lively baby.

Mrs Catkin wanted to visit her sister, but she couldn't take an elephant with her.

And she couldn't find anyone in the village to look after Daisy. They all said an elephant was too big and too tricky.

She looked over the fence and saw Benny trying to wash the lawn.

'I've got an odd job for you,' she said. 'I must go and see my sister and I want you to look after my baby elephant.'

Benny was thrilled.

'Hooray!' he sang out, and skipped round in a little circle.

That's why he only heard half of
what Mrs Catkin told him. He heard her
say 'sister' and he heard her say 'look
after' and he heard her say 'baby'. The
rest he missed.

'She can stay in your shed,' said Mrs
Catkin, 'and she likes a bun now and
then. And you will be nice to her, won't
you, Benny?'

'Of course!' said Benny, bouncing up
and down.

'Good. I'll bring her round tomorrow.'

Mrs Catkin went home and Benny rushed in to tell Bob the good news. Bob was thrilled too. He and Benny danced round the kitchen, and bubbles and foam flew all over the place. It was a messy dance, but they didn't mind mess.

'But what is this job?' asked Bob, stopping suddenly.

Benny screwed up his eyes and thought hard. What was it Mrs Catkin had told him?

'I know,' he said at last. 'We have to look after Mrs Catkin's baby sister. She can stay in our bed and she likes the sun.'

'Are you sure?'

'Almost certainly,' said Benny.

'Then let's get ready,' said Bob.

Their own bed didn't look soft enough for Mrs Catkin's baby sister, so they found some cushions and piled them on top.

'She should be happy on that,' said Bob when they'd finished.

'She should be very happy on that,' said Benny.

Daisy

When Benny and Bob opened the door next morning, they staggered back in surprise at what they saw. Mrs Catkin smiled and held out a note.

'I've put the instructions in this note,' she said.

But Bob was too shocked to answer her.

'Benny,' he whispered, 'there's an elephant on our doorstep.'

Benny could see that. He screwed up
his eyes and tried to remember what
Mrs Catkin had said to him yesterday.

'I think this must be Mrs Catkin's
baby sister,' he whispered back.

'It *can't* be. It's an elephant.'

'This is Daisy,' said Mrs Catkin.
'And she's looking forward to staying
with you.'

She gave Daisy a pat, put the note
on the mat and turned to walk away.

Bob and Benny were too stunned to say goodbye. They stared at Daisy with their mouths open.

'Benny,' said Bob, 'you're a clot.'

'It was your idea to do odd jobs,' said Benny. 'You're the clot.'

For some moments they stood on the step, trying to knock each other's hat off. Daisy watched them with interest. When their row was over, Bob said they ought to bring her indoors.

'After all,' he said, 'she is our guest.'

So they squeezed her through the door and led her into the house. Daisy liked the look of it. It wasn't too tidy and there were lots of interesting things she could pick up with her trunk.

'This is your bed, Miss Catkin,' said Benny when they got to the bedroom.

Daisy liked the look of the bed, too. She picked up some of the cushions and flung them around.

Then she put a foot on the mattress to test it out. There was a twanging sound and the bed fell in.

'Are you sure she has to sleep in our bed?' said Bob.

'Yes,' said Benny. 'Bed and sun, that's what Mrs Catkin said. I think.'

'Well there's no sun in here, so we must think of something else.'

Finding the sun

After a while Bob had a good idea.

'We must put the bed on the lawn,' he said. 'So it can get the sun.'

'Excellent,' said Benny.

Some ideas are simple to think of but hard to carry out. This was one of them.

Bob and Benny tried to lift the bed. One stood at the top and the other at the bottom. Bob and Benny heaved and heaved but it didn't move, not even a tiny bit.

'Maybe,' said Benny, 'we should ask
Daisy to get off.'

'For once you've thought of
something useful,' Bob said.

They talked to Daisy in soft, sweet
voices but she took no notice. She liked
Bob and Benny's bed. She was happy
there. All she needed was a bun to
make it perfect.

'This is no good,' said Benny. 'We can't lift the bed with an elephant on it. You'll have to think of something else.'

So Bob scratched his head and tried to think of another idea.

'We can't get the bed into the garden,' he said, 'so what must we do?'

'Bring the garden to the bed,' said Benny.

'Clot. If we did that, where would the sun be?'

'Where it always is. Outside.'

'So what must we do?'

'Bring the sun inside.'

'Yes. Exactly.'

Benny was pleased to be right, but he didn't know how they were going to bring the sun into the bedroom.

'That's easy,' said Bob. 'We'll make a hole in the roof!'

On the roof

Bob and Benny went outside to fetch
the ladder. Daisy stayed on the bed.
She was quite comfortable but she
missed them. They were kind to her
and they made her laugh, in an
elephant sort of way.

She looked out of the window and
saw them struggling with the ladder.
They tottered backwards and forwards,
trying to lean it against the house.

Then she saw them climb the ladder, disappear on to the roof, and she was alone again. Alone and hungry. She looked around the bedroom. Not a bun in sight. The cushions looked a bit like buns but they were really too big and too dry.

I'll have to go and look for one, she thought.

So she got up and wandered through the house.

Meanwhile,
Bob and Benny
were at work
on the roof.
They had a hard time of it because it
started to rain.

'This is no good,' said Benny. 'The
sun's gone.'

'Never mind,' Bob said. 'We must
carry on.'

They pulled some tiles off and
hammered away at the plaster. It was
messy work, but they didn't mind mess.

When they'd made a good big
hole, Bob sent Benny back
down the ladder.

21

'See what it looks like from the bedroom,' he told him.

Down went Benny and minutes later he stood in the bedroom.

'There are plaster and puddles everywhere,' he called up to Bob.

'Never mind that. Can you see the sky?'

'Yes.'

'And can you see it from the bed?'

'Yes.'

'And does Daisy like it?'

'I don't know.'

'Why not?'

'Because she's not here.'

'WHAT?'

Bob was shocked. He slipped on the
wet roof and fell through the hole,
landing on the pile of cushions. He
bounced lightly up and down until, little
by little, he came to rest.

'That was lucky,' Benny said.

'It was NOT lucky,' said Bob. 'I just fell
through the roof.'

'But you didn't land on Daisy, did you?'

Bob jumped up. Of course! He didn't
land on Daisy, because Daisy wasn't there.

'We have to find her,' he snapped.
'Quick, Benny! Get looking!'

Benny picked up some cushions and looked under them. He moved the clock and looked behind it.

'Not in here!' said Bob. 'We must search the whole house!'

They ran through every room in the house, calling for Daisy, but she was nowhere to be found.

Where is Daisy?

Then Benny saw the letter on the door-mat.

'Oh, look,' he said. 'She's left a note.'

'Don't be silly,' said Bob. 'She can't write. She's only a baby.'

'Well, someone's left a note.'

Bob picked it up and read it. It was the note Mrs Catkin had left.

'Dear Bob and Benny,

Don't forget: be nice to Daisy. She can sleep in your shed and she likes plenty of buns.'

'Shed and buns,' said Bob, shaking the note at Benny. 'Not bed and sun!'

'Well, I was nearly right,' said Benny.

'You clot! Why didn't you listen?'

'And why didn't you pick the note up? You're the clot!'

'Oh, no!' said Bob. 'Look! The front door's still open.'

'Perhaps she's popped out to the baker's,' said Benny. 'To get some buns.'

'Yes!' said Bob. 'Brilliant! Come on!'

Out they ran and up the street to the baker's, calling Daisy's name as they went. And – thank goodness – there she was, safe and sound, picking buns off the baker's shelf with her trunk.

Bob and Benny danced with joy at the sight of her.

And Daisy did a much heavier dance
at the sight of the buns. The only one
who wasn't dancing was the baker.

'Look at it!' he shouted. 'Look at it!
It's shoplifting!'

But he calmed down when Bob paid
him for the buns and they led Daisy
out of his shop.

They put the cushions in their shed
and Daisy went in after them. She fitted
very nicely, and, with the door open,
she had a good view of the garden.

In the afternoon the rain stopped and she watched Bob and Benny mow the lawn. Then they got her to walk up and down to make the lawn flat. Daisy enjoyed that. She liked to be useful. They gave her the grass clippings on a big dish with a bun on top, and she enjoyed that, too.

When Mrs Catkin came back from her sister's, she was delighted to see Daisy looking so well.

'You've done a very good job, boys,' she said, and she paid them well.

With the money they bought two large umbrellas. When the rain came back that night, they lay in bed with the umbrellas up. They dozed off to the sound of the rain pattering on the umbrellas. It was still a bit messy, but they didn't mind mess.

About the author

While I was teaching,
I enjoyed drama and reading
books aloud with children.
This encouraged me to write
and since then I have written
a number of scripts for radio,
stage and television, around
a baker's dozen or so – that

is, thirteen – children's books. Sad to say,
I am not good at odd jobs of any kind. When
I was thirteen I made a table at school, but it
fell off the bus on the way home and one of
its legs came off.

I enjoy reading, almost anything to do
with cricket, and cycling around Cambridge,
where I live with my family.

An Odd Job for

Bob and Benny

NICK WARBURTON

Illustrated by Wendy Smith

OXFORD
UNIVERSITY PRESS

OXFORD
UNIVERSITY PRESS

Great Clarendon Street, Oxford OX2 6DP

Oxford University Press is a department of the University of Oxford.
It furthers the University's objective of excellence in research, scholarship,
and education by publishing worldwide in

Oxford   New York

Auckland   Cape Town   Dar es Salaam   Hong Kong   Karachi
Kuala Lumpur   Madrid   Melbourne   Mexico City   Nairobi
New Delhi   Shanghai   Taipei   Toronto

With offices in

Argentina   Austria   Brazil   Chile   Czech Republic   France   Greece
Guatemala   Hungary   Italy   Japan   Poland   Portugal   Singapore
South Korea   Switzerland   Thailand   Turkey   Ukraine   Vietnam

Oxford is a registered trade mark of Oxford University Press
in the UK and in certain other countries

British Library Cataloguing in Publication Data
Data available

ISBN 978-0-19-917986-2

17 19 20 18 16

Available in packs
Stage 11 More Stories A Pack of 6:
ISBN 978-0-19-917983-1
Stage 11 More Stories A Class Pack:
ISBN 978-0-19-917990-9
Guided Reading Cards also available:
ISBN 978-0-19-917992-3

Cover artwork by Wendy Smith
Photograph of Nick Warburton © Eaden Lilley Photography, Cambridge

Printed in China by Imago

Paper used in the production of this book is a natural,
recyclable product made from wood grown in sustainable forests.
The manufacturing process conforms to the environmental
regulations of the country of origin.